THE SECOND STREET SNOOPS

*For Andrew —
Have fun!

Nancy Swettord
(Grama Nancy)*

To all my grandchildren, especially those
who love to play with words - Grama Nancy

The Second Street Snoops

© Nancy Sweetland 2008
Illustrations by the author

This book is a work of fiction. All characters and incidents are the product of the author's imagination. Any resemblance to actual events or places or persons, living or dead, is entirely coincidental.

Published by
Lighthouse Christian Publishing
SAN 257-4330
5531 Dufferin Drive
Savage, Minnesota, 55378
United States of America

www.lighthouseebooks.com
www.lighthousechristianpublishing.com

The Stories

The Mystery of the Missing A 2

The Mystery of the Missing Bees 18

The Mystery of the Missing Key 41

The Mystery of the Colorful Cat 60

The Mystery of the Buffalo Button ... 83

The Mystery of the Missing L 101

The Case of the Disappearing
Dinosaur Egg 113

The Mystery of the Sticks in the
Sanctuary 141

THE SECOND STREET SNOOPS AND THE MYSTERY OF THE MISSING "A"

CHAPTER ONE

"We're going to be detectives," announced Alfie and Betts Binks on the first morning of summer vacation.

"That's nice," said Mrs. Binks. "Finish your pancakes, please."

Mr. Binks said "Hmmm" from behind the morning paper.

"We're serious," said Betts.

"Like Sherlock Holmes and Watson," added Alfie.

"Without the pipe, I hope," said Mr. Binks.

"Which one of you is Sherlock?"

"We'll take turns," said Betts. "I'm not doing all the paperwork."

Mrs. Binks went to work at the library where she volunteered. Mr. Binks went to work at the bank. Alfie and Betts went to work making a colorful sign to put in the front window.

DETECTING DONE HERE

The Second Street Snoops

**YOU HAVE A MYSTERY?
WE'LL MAKE IT
HISTORY!**

They waited. People walked by.

"I guess it takes time to get customers," said Alfie.

Just then the phone rang.

"Second Street Snoops," answered Betts in her best business voice.

It was their mom, Mrs. Binks. "I have a mystery for you. The library sign is missing its letter A."

"We'll be right there!" said Betts.

CHAPTER TWO

The shiny sign in front of the library read:

"The letter A was here yesterday," said Mrs. Binks. "I know, because the sign was spattered with mud. I asked the janitor to clean it and I'm sure he would have told us if the A had been missing then. Well, I must get back to work. Good luck, Snoops."

"Hmmm." Alfie ran his hand over the sign. "Yuk! It's all slimy." He wiped his hand on his jeans. Then he looked carefully at the ground through his large, round magnifying glass. "Make a note, Betts. No footprints."

"No footprints," said Betts, writing in a small notebook.

"Nothing else missing," said Alfie.

'Nothing else missing,' wrote Betts.

"No witnesses," said Alfie.

'Need a witness,' wrote Betts. "I'm getting writer's cramp. Next time, *I'm* Sherlock."

A large St. Bernard dog bounded up to them. He licked Alfie's hand. He tried to lick Betts' face. He sniffed all around the library sign and licked it too, leaving stringy slobbers of dog drool. Then he loped away into the woods behind the library.

"The criminal always returns to the scene of the crime," said Alfie.

"That dog is a criminal?" asked Betts.

"Everything is important in an investigation," said Alfie. "Dogs have a great sense of smell. Maybe his nose knows something we don't. Make a note."

Betts wrote, "Dog's nose knows." She frowned. "Sure. But how's he going to tell us?"

CHAPTER THREE

Inside the library, Alfie asked Miss Page, the librarian, "Is anything else missing?"

"Yes," said Miss Page. "When I got home, my spray shortening wasn't in the grocery bag that I'd put into the janitor's closet."

"Hmmm," said Alfie. "That's interesting. Betts, make a note. There could be a connection here."

'Short shortening,' wrote Betts. "I'm hungry. Let's go home and connect with some food."

A thin old man was waiting on their front

step.

"I'm Henry Bell," he said. "Think you detectives can help me find my friend Frank? He's been gone two days."

'Find Frank,' wrote Betts. "He hasn't called?"

"Not likely. He can't talk," said Henry Bell.

'Can't talk,' wrote Betts.

"What's he look like?" asked Alfie.

"Big. Brown and white. Friendly. Drools a lot," said Henry Bell.

'Friendly. Drools,' wrote Betts, nodding at Alfie. "I think we have a clue."

CHAPTER FOUR

Alfie and Betts made peanut butter and pickle sandwiches and ate them in their backyard swing.

"We know that the Saint Bernard must be called Frank," said Betts, chewing away. "If we can't find the library's A, at least we can find Henry Bell's dog."

"Uh-huh." Alfie nodded. "And I think if we find Frank, we'll find the missing letter A. Did you watch him at that sign?"

Alfie took another bite of his sandwich and chewed slowly, thinking hard. "We need to connect the evidence, like Sherlock Holmes would."

Betts flipped through her notes. "What evidence? I don't see how anything connects."

"Check the notes you took at the library, Watson. But first, let's find Frank." Alfie started toward the house. "We'll take that ham bone from last night's dinner."

Alfie put the bone in a plastic bag and stuffed it in his pocket. They biked to the woods where the Saint Bernard had gone.

Betts stopped and shook her head. "I don't want to go in there."

"Come on, don't be a sissy. We've got a job to do." Pulling Betts along, Alfie plunged into the thick bushes.

They searched for a long time. Betts found an old tennis ball. Alfie found a piece of rope. They didn't find Frank.

"Listen!" said Betts, grabbing Alfie's arm. "Something big is coming!"

CHAPTER FIVE

They jumped onto an enormous fallen log.

CRASH! SMASH! A huge black dog burst out of the bushes. It wasn't Frank. And it wasn't friendly.

The dog growled. He pawed the ground. He barked, showing jagged teeth and a dripping red tongue. He hurled himself at the log. He almost reached Alfie's foot.

"Don't move, Betts," said Alfie. His voice shook.

"I couldn't move if I wanted to," said Betts,

clutching Alfie's arm. Her teeth chattered.

The dog growled and pawed the ground with one leg. He snarled and threw himself at them again.

A frightened rabbit leaped from under the log and streaked away through the bushes. A split second later the dog bounded after it.

Betts jumped to the ground. "I'm getting out of here! Coming, Sherlock?"

She tripped over a branch and fell face down in a pile of leaves. She heard snorts and felt hot, wet breath on the back of her neck.

"Help! Alfie!" she yelled. "It's got me!"

CHAPTER SIX

Alfie laughed. "Don't panic, Watson! I think we've found Frank."

Betts sat up and pushed the Saint Bernard away. "I think *he* found *us*. And boy, he *does* drool!"

"Slobber's more like it. Lucky I found this rope." He tied it to Frank's collar. "Now Frank can help us solve the other mystery."

Betts got up, brushing dirt off her jeans. "Sure. You ask him questions, and I'll write down his answers. Then we'll put his paw print on it for a signature!"

"I'm serious." Alfie held the ham bone to Frank's wet nose. "Hang on, I think Frank's about to show us something pretty interesting, aren't you, Frank?"

Frank grabbed the bone in his mouth and took off, dragging Alfie behind him. Betts ran to keep up.

Frank ran deeper into the woods, sniffing the ground. Then he stopped and began to dig.

"I thought so," said Alfie, nodding. "Watch!"

CHAPTER SEVEN

Frank's scrabbling paws threw leaves and dirt in all directions.

Something else came flying up out of the hole.

"It's the Library's letter A!" said Betts. She picked it up to brush it off. "Frank buried it! Why?"

Alfie grinned. "Elementary, my dear Watson. It smelled like something to eat."

Betts made a face. "I don't get it."

"Last night the bank janitor sprayed the sign with Miss Page's shortening instead of cleaner."

"And you know that because . . . ?" Betts frowned.

"Because the sign was all slimy, remember?"

Betts flipped through her notebook. "I see. Frank licked the sign because it smelled like food. The A was loose, and he knocked it off. Then he buried it. Just like the bone."

"Right. And as Sherlock would say, the game was afoot." Alfie grinned. "Only, in this case, it was *under*foot. Come on, let's take that letter A back to the library. Then we'll take Frank home to Henry Bell. I think we've done enough detecting for one day."

Betts nodded. "Good work." She pushed her notebook into her back pocket. "Cases closed. But next time *I* get to be Sherlock."

The End

THE SECOND STREET SNOOPS AND THE MYSTERY OF THE MISSING BEES

CHAPTER ONE

After Mrs. Binks had gone to the library where she volunteered, and Mr. Binks had gone to the Wayside bank where he loaned people money, Alfie and Betts Binks sat on their front steps hoping for a mystery to solve. They were spending their summer vacation being detectives like Sherlock Holmes and Watson.

"We'll take turns being Sherlock," Betts had said. "I'm not doing all the paperwork."

In the window behind them hung their large, red-bordered sign:

> **DETECTING DONE HERE**
>
> **The Second Street Snoops**
>
> **YOU HAVE A MYSTERY? WE'LL MAKE IT HISTORY!**

"Now there's something interesting!" Betts pointed down the street. "Look!"

A rickety, rusty pickup truck screeched slowly to a halt at their house.

"For sure," agreed Alfie. "Maybe that old man reading our sign has a mystery for us."

"I hope so. It's been awfully quiet since we found Henry Bell's dog and the letter A from the library sign," said Betts.

A gnarly old man got slowly out of his truck

and put on his crumpled leather hat. From its uneven brim, netting hung down to cover his shoulders.

"Now, there's a mystery already," said Alfie.

"Not really," said Betts. "That's a bee-keepers hat. It's to keep him from getting stung. Remember, if he's got a mystery for us, this time I'm Sherlock."

"How could I forget?" Alfie sighed. "You keep reminding me."

The old man lifted the netting away from his face as he shuffled toward them. He wore baggy farmer overalls and high-top rubber boots. His worried face was lined with wrinkles.

"Just came from the bank," he said in a voice as creaky as his truck. "Your Dad said I'd find you detectives hereabouts. Said you found something for the library, and for Henry Bell, too."

"Yes, sir." Alfie and Betts stood up.

Betts asked, "How can we help you?"

"Not likely you two know anythin' about

bees." The old man squinted at Betts first, then Alfie. "Do you?"

Betts said, "I know they pollinate plants."

Alfie added, "And they make honey."

The old man frowned. "Guess that's a start. Well, my bees are gone. Just gone. Your Dad says maybe you can find 'em."

Alfie and Betts grinned at each other. Betts said, "Take a note, Watson. Bees gone."

Alfie pulled a stubby pencil and a small notebook out of his back pocket and wrote, 'Bees gone.'

"Your name, sir?" Betts asked. "For our records."

"Suppose you'll send a bill. Well, I won't pay unless you get 'em back, understand," the old man grumbled. "Name's Horton. Horton's Heavenly Honey. Maybe you've heard of it. Anyways, try some."

He pulled a small jar out of his overalls pocket and held it out. The sun shone golden through the liquid inside.

"Thanks, Mr. Horton," said Betts, taking the jar. "We love honey. Now give us the details. Just how many bees are we talking about? And when and where were they last seen?"

CHAPTER TWO

"Tell you on the way. Best if I take you with me," said Mr. Horton. "Show you my empty hive. Call your Dad, make sure it's okay. He knows me. Fact, he's got my loan for the shed. Lose my bees, and I won't be able to pay for that shed, neither. Comin'?"

"You bet!" Alfie said, stuffing the little notebook back in his pocket. "Just wait 'til I call Dad."

A few minutes later they climbed into the rickety truck for the short drive to Mr. Horton's small farm only a few minutes from the Binks' house on Second Street. As they rattled into the bumpy yard beside Mr. Horton's trailer house about a dozen red and white chickens scattered, squawking, in all directions.

Mr. Horton stamped on the brake pedal. The brakes screeched and sent the chickens flapping even more wildly.

"Now, how'd they get out? I know I shut that gate to the chicken yard when I fed 'em this morning. First thing you know they'll be gone, too."

Alfie and Betts looked at each other.

Alfie whispered, "Sabotage?"

Betts nodded. "Could be," she whispered back. "But why?"

Then they said together, "We'll help you catch your chickens, Mr. Horton."

Twenty minutes later, with all the chickens noisily squawking inside their fenced yard, Mr. Horton shook his head. "Just look at this," he said, holding a broken piece of wire in his hand. "This hook is broke right off. Old wire musta' been rustier than I thought."

"Let me see that, please," said Betts. She examined the wire with their large magnifying glass. "It's pretty old, all right," she said quietly to Alfie. "But it looks like it might have been cut. Make a note, Watson."

Alfie wrote, 'Wire may be cut.'

Betts looked from the piece of wire to Mr. Horton's neat trailer house surrounded by a small, trimmed yard edged with blooming pansies. "Has there been anything else missing from your farm lately, Mr. Horton?" she asked.

Mr. Horton pulled off his veiled hat and shook his grey head. "Don't think so. Man my age misplaces things sometimes, finds 'em later. Still lookin' for that sandwich I put down somewhere yesterday."

Alfie made an entry in his notebook. 'Missing sandwich.' "What kind?" he asked curiously.

"Why, peanut butter and honey. Always have that for lunch," said Mr. Horton. "Best honey in the world, Horton's Honey. Lots better than Bunny's Honey. That's too runny. Silly name, too."

Alfie made a note, 'Sandwich peanut butter and honey. Horton's better than Bunny's runny honey.'

"I meant something a little more important," said Betts. "Something like... like... money. Or maybe, tools missing."

"Not so's I noticed. Come on, I'll show you where my bees ought to be."

Mr. Horton shuffled ahead of them toward the grove of trees behind his trailer house, where a grey box like a small dresser about three feet tall with closed drawers stood in an open space. There were no bees anywhere near it.

"Hmmm," said Betts. "They were here yesterday?" She walked carefully all around the hive, studying the ground.

"Sure were. Buzzin' around like crazy."

Alfie made a note: 'Bees buzzing yesterday like crazy.' "See anything?" he asked.

"Just this," said Betts, pointing. "Here in the dirt. It's a footprint. Looks like a boot. Pointy toe, like a cowboy boot."

"Yeah," said Alfie. He wrote, 'Pointy-toe boot print in dirt.'

"Um-hmmm," said Betts. "This mystery is *definitely* afoot."

CHAPTER THREE

"Do you know anyone who wears cowboy boots, Mr. Horton?" asked Betts.

Mr. Horton frowned. "Could be. Never noticed."

"All right if I take a look inside?" asked Alfie, pointing to the deserted hive.

"Can't hurt now." Mr. Horton lifted off a heavy lead weight that held down the hive cover. Inside a number of wooden racks stood on end. He pulled one up to show how the honeycomb filled each slat. "See? Not a bee around . . . and this honeycomb's only part filled. My queen's gone and the whole swarm — that's what they call all the bees — went with her. So, think you can find my bees?"

Alfie made a note. 'Queen gone. Swarm gone.'

"We certainly will try, but we need to do some research," said Betts. "Please give us a ride home. We'll get back to you as soon as we can."

At their house, Alfie and Betts each made a peanut butter and Horton's Heavenly Honey sandwich on whole-wheat bread. They put them with two shiny red apples and tall glasses of milk on a tray and carried it out to the shady backyard swing.

"What have we got?" asked Betts, through a mouthful of sandwich.

Alfie read his notebook entries. "Not much. I thought I'd learn something from the encyclopedia, but it says when the queen goes, they all go. That's a fact. We have to find out why she went."

"And where. Did she go on her own? Or did somebody take her?"

"Would you take a queen bee anywhere if you thought five thousand other bees would chase you?" asked Alfie.

"Nooooo . . . not unless . . ." Betts stopped.

"Unless what?" Alfie asked, his sandwich halfway to his mouth.

"Unless I wanted Mr. Horton's Heavenly Honey off the market."

Alfie squinted. "Yeah, Sherlock. Good thinking. You might do that if your honey wasn't as good."

"Right! If, for instance, your honey was runny."

Alfie stuffed his apple into his pocket. "Let's make a visit to . . ." he paused.

"Bunny's runny honey!" finished Betts. "And we just might take a look at Honey Bunny's boots, if we can."

CHAPTER FOUR

Alfie and Betts pedaled their bright red ten-speed bikes past the bank where Mr. Binks worked, and waved through the library window at Mrs. Binks on their way to the Bunny's Honey Farm.

A sign showing a big blue rabbit holding up a jar of bright yellow honey marked the start of a long, tree-covered driveway. Betts peered down the road.

"I can see a house," she said. "Looks creepy."

"How creepy can a honey-maker's house be?" asked Alfie. "C'mon."

They pedaled slowly into the dense stand of trees that completely shut away the sun. The only sound was their bike tires whispering on gravel.

"What if we do find a bunch of bees?" asked Alfie. "Can you tell one from another? How would we know Mr. Horton's from regular Bunny's Honey bees?"

"Good question," answered Betts. "Right now we're just checking things out. We don't even know who Bunny is, yet."

A tiny cottage with a high, pointed roof stood in a small clearing in the woods. The shutters and the chimney were painted bright pink. The rest of the cottage was the same brilliant blue as the rabbit on the Bunny's Honey sign.

"Wow," breathed Betts as they got closer. "I told you it was creepy. It looks like the witch's house in Hansel and Gretel!"

"Yeah," said Alfie. "And I don't like it. Let's go."

They turned their bikes around, but just then the top half of the bright pink door burst open and a short, plump woman leaned out. "Hello, dears! Have you come for Bunny's Honey? Come right in." Her high voice went up and down like a song. "I'm Honey Bunny. Sonny Bunny's doing chores in the barn, but I can help you, I'm sure."

Alfie and Betts looked at each other. Betts said in a low voice, "We did take the case, after all."

"Yeah we did," said Alfie. "And I'm beginning

to wish we hadn't."

They parked their bikes and walked slowly to the door, where Betts introduced them politely and said, "We're interested in honey bees, and we wondered if we could see your hives. So we know what they look like."

Mrs. Bunny smiled widely. "What a good idea! I was just going out to look at them myself. We added a second hive a couple of days ago, but we haven't filled it yet, so you can see how a hive looks before and after the bees are in it."

She chattered cheerily on about how nice it was to see young people interested in bee-keeping as she pushed open the bottom half of the pink door and stepped out.

Betts elbowed Alfie's ribs and whispered, "See if you can check her shoes."

"Foiled." Alfie said, shaking his head. "Her long dress reaches the ground."

But then Honey Bunny nearly tripped and clutched at her skirt, holding it up for just a

The Second Street Snoops

moment. "Foiled again," muttered Alfie. "She's wearing high top tennies."

CHAPTER FIVE

Disappointed, Alfie and Betts walked behind Honey Bunny to an open area behind her barn. There, in the bright sunshine, were two hives . . . and both of them were full of busy bees.

"Why, I never!" Mrs. Bunny said, covering her mouth with her hand and stepping backward so quickly she almost fell over. "Where did that swarm come from? We don't have that many bees!"

Betts helped her catch her balance and whispered to Alfie, "They must be Mr. Horton's.

She really acts innocent. Make a note."

Alfie pulled out his pencil and notebook and wrote, 'Mrs. Bunny surprised. Extra bees. Many extra.'

With a bang, the barn door flew open and Sonny Bunny ran into the clearing. "Hey! What are these kids doing here, Ma?"

"Why, Sonny, they're interested in bees, so I'm showing them the hives . . . but look!" She pointed. "The new hive is full! Where did these bees come from?"

He didn't answer.

Betts and Alfie stared at Sonny Bunny's feet. At Sonny Bunny's cowboy boots.

"I can tell you, Mrs. Bunny," said Betts, bravely. "Those are Mr. Horton's bees. And you," she pointed her finger at Sonny Bunny, "you took them from Mr. Horton. How did you do it?"

"Sonny, you didn't!" Mrs. Bunny exclaimed. "You wouldn't!"

Sonny Bunny hung his head and kicked a

stick with the toe of his cowboy boot. "Yeah, Ma, I did," he confessed. "I took the smoker over to his place the other day when he was gone. I let his chickens loose so he wouldn't think about his bees while I settled them down with the smoke. Then I took the queen and the whole swarm came real easy."

Mrs. Bunny stared at her son. "But why would you do such a thing?"

Sonny kept looking at the ground, digging at the dirt with his pointy-toed boot. "I thought if I took his bees, we'd get good honey like his that sells better. I didn't think anybody'd know. He'd just think they swarmed away by themselves."

"But your honey would sell better if it just wasn't so runny. Mr. Horton said so," said Alfie, standing very straight. "You didn't need to steal his bees."

"Really?" Sonny Bunny looked surprised. "It doesn't sell because it's runny?" He frowned. "Maybe I shouldn't add that water to it. But it does make more."

"You've been adding water to our honey, Sonny? Well, I never! No wonder it didn't sell! Now you'd just better get the smoker and take those bees right back where they belong!" Mrs. Bunny said, shaking her finger at her son. "And I'll deal with you later!"

Back at home, Alfie labeled his notebook *The Case of the Missing Bees* and filed it next to *The Case of the Missing A* on the top shelf of the bookcase.

"Good work, Sherlock!" he said, giving Betts a high five.

"Elementary, my dear Watson," Betts answered. "It was a sticky case, but it's closed. And next time you get to be Sherlock."

The End

THE SECOND STREET SNOOPS AND THE MYSTERY OF THE MISSING KEY

CHAPTER ONE

"Finding Mr. Horton's missing bees was fun, wasn't it?" Betts asked, putting the Toasty Oats box in the cupboard. She and Alfie were cleaning up the kitchen after Monday morning breakfast.

"Yes," answered Alfie, handing her a bowl to put into the dishwasher. "Seeing all those bees in their hive was special, too. Being detectives lets us learn lots of things we wouldn't otherwise."

"That's true. I wonder what our next mystery will be."

"I hope there's one soon," said Alfie. "It's my

turn to be Sherlock." He put the milk into the refrigerator.

Just then the phone rang. "That's a mystery ring, I just know it!" said Betts. She ran to the phone. "Binks residence," she answered in her most grown-up manner.

"Is this the Second Street Snoops?" asked a booming, familiar-sounding voice.

Betts held the telephone away from her ear and mouthed to Alfie, "It's Pastor Perkins!" Then she said, "Yes it is, Pastor Perkins. What can we do for you?"

"My! You really *are* a detective," he said. "How did you know it was me?"

Betts laughed. "We hear your voice every Sunday at church, Pastor, that's how. Do you have a mystery for us?"

"I wish I didn't but I'm afraid I do. Could you detectives come to the rectory this morning? I have a problem here that needs some snooping into."

"We'll bike right over, Pastor," said Betts. "Give us fifteen minutes."

CHAPTER TWO

"Poor Pastor Perkins," said Alfie as they pedaled toward the church. "He's always knocking something over or losing something. Remember that Sunday when he couldn't find his glasses to read his sermon?"

Betts giggled. "They were on top of his head the whole time."

"Yeah. And yesterday after church when everyone was at the social? He spilled his whole cup of coffee right down the front of his suit." Alfie grinned. "What a mess! Lucky for him, Mrs.

Perkins had already gone home."

"He's probably misplaced something, or can't find his Bible," said Betts. "C'mon, let's find out."

They parked their bikes in the rack by the church and walked around the building to the rectory.

"Well, good morning!" Mrs. Perkins answered the door with a smile. "Pastor told me he'd asked you to come, but he wouldn't say what for." She ushered them into the house. Then she whispered, "I think he's lost something again. I hope you can help. He's got himself in quite a state."

Pastor Perkins looked up from his big, cluttered desk when Alfie knocked politely on his open door. His white hair stood in clumps as if he'd been running both hands through it. "Ah, Binks and Binks, detectives!" he said. "Thank you for coming so quickly."

"Yes, sir. What can we help you with?" Alfie asked.

"Sit down, sit down." Pastor Perkins gestured to the two chairs that faced his desk. That's right, take a load off, as my grandma used to say. How have you been?"

"We just saw you yesterday, Pastor. We're fine," said Betts.

"Oh, of course," said the Pastor. "I know. I'm just making small talk. Let's get down to business."

CHAPTER THREE

"What business are we getting down to, Pastor?" Betts asked. She pulled her small notebook and a stubby pencil out of her jeans pocket and got ready to write. "Do you have a problem?"

"Yes. Yes, I certainly do." He got up and closed the study door. "Shhh. I don't want Mrs. Perkins to know about it," he said in a whisper. "She thinks I'm getting forgetful. She may be right but I don't want to admit it." He walked toward a large door in the wall. "See this?" He rattled the doorknob and pulled but the door stayed firmly closed. "*This* is my problem. I have to write my sermon for next Sunday and I can't get into this closet where I keep all my reference books. Even my study Bible is in there!"

"Is it locked?" Alfie asked. "Or just stuck?"

"Oh, it's locked," said Pastor Perkins. "I locked it myself. And now I can't find the key."

"Make a note, Watson," said Alfie.

Betts nodded and wrote, 'Books in locked closet. No key to missing key.'

Pastor Perkins wrung his hands. "I *must* get to my books! I suppose it's silly to lock them up, but they're really important to me. Oh, Snoops, I have faith that you can find that key."

"We'll certainly try," said Alfie. "When did you have it last?"

"Just yesterday after church when I put my books away, but for the life of me I can't find it now." He patted his pockets. "I remember slipping it into my pocket, where I always keep it. Or I think I remember doing that. But it's not there." He slumped into his chair. "If I tell Mrs. Perkins she'll turn the house upside down—and me, too—looking for it." He ran his fingers through his hair again. "Oh, dear, I can't write my sermon without my reference books." He thought for a moment. "Well, maybe I could but it would be very short."

Alfie wondered if that would be such a bad thing, but he didn't say so out loud. He went over to the closet and tried to open it himself, but it didn't budge. "How large is the key, Pastor?" he asked. "Is it silver or brass?"

"It's brass, kind of fancy. Old Fashioned, you know? About this big." He held his thumb and index finger about three inches apart.

'Three inch key. Fancy brass,' wrote Betts. "That's not very big," she said. "It could be anywhere." She wrote, 'Could be anywhere.'

"And that's my problem," moaned Pastor Perkins. "Anywhere at all."

CHAPTER FOUR

Pastor Perkins got up from his chair. "I have an errand to do and then I must go to the hospital and visit old Mrs. Jones. She fell and broke her hip. So go to it, Snoops. I have faith that you'll find my key!" He buttoned his suit coat and went out.

"Wow," said Alfie, looking around Pastor Perkin's cluttered office. "Where shall we start?"

"How about starting in the kitchen with milk and some peanut-butter cookies I just took out of the oven?" asked Mrs. Perkins from the door. "Then you can start to do whatever it is that

Pastor is so worked up about. And you don't even have to tell me what it is."

Alfie and Betts followed her into the kitchen. She poured them each a glass of milk.

"These cookies are just heavenly!" said Alfie, munching away.

"As they should be in a church rectory," said Betts, grinning. "Mrs. Perkins, has the Pastor been acting funny since yesterday at all?"

"Funnier than usual?" she asked, smiling. "Pastor always acts funny after Sunday church. He's so happy to be done with giving a sermon for another week. But then right away he starts worrying about what he'll sermonize about the next week. It's very upsetting for him when he can't get started on Monday."

"Hmmm," said Betts, reaching for another cookie. "We'll do our best to help him out."

"He was sure you would." Mrs. Perkins poured them both another glass of milk and went outside to work in her garden.

CHAPTER FIVE

"Well," said Alfie, "What do you think?"

"I think," said Betts, "that we're missing some important information."

"Like what?"

"Like what did Pastor Perkins do with his suit coat when he got home? If he tossed it over a chair, or something like that, the key could have fallen out."

Alfie nodded. "Maybe. But I have an idea. Come with me."

Betts followed Alfie into the garden. "Mrs.

Perkins," said Alfie, "I hate to bother you, but can you tell us where Pastor's suit coat is? The one he had on yesterday at church?"

Mrs. Perkins frowned. "No, I haven't seen it. Why?"

Betts wrote, 'Mrs. P hasn't seen coat.'

"Just wondering. We'll be back soon. If Pastor Perkins comes home before we get here, tell him we're on the case."

Mrs. Perkins smiled. "I'm sure you are." She went back to pulling weeds. As they were leaving, she called after them, "I hope you can solve it!"

They pulled their bikes from the rack. "I hope so, too," said Betts. "Pastor Perkins has faith that we will."

"I think we already have," said Alfie.

"Okay, Sherlock, give. What do you know that I don't?"

Alfie hopped on his bike and gestured for Betts to do the same.

"Where are we going?" she asked as they

pedaled toward downtown. "What's the key to the key?"

Alfie grinned. "Remember that Pastor Perkins spilled all that coffee on his suit yesterday?"

"Sure. But so what?" Betts frowned. "Slow down, for pete's sake."

Alfie slowed down. "Think about it. What do you do with clothes that are stained?"

"Take them to the...oho!" Betts said.

Alfie finished her sentence, "Right! To the dry cleaners! You've got it! I'm thinking that Pastor Perkin's errand this morning was to do just that, so Mrs. Perkins wouldn't know he'd spilled the coffee."

"And the key is still in that suit pocket," finished Betts. "The pocket's got it! I'll write that note as soon as we have the key."

At the dry cleaners Alfie asked, "Did Pastor Perkins just drop off a suit coat here?"

"Why, yes, he did," said the clerk. "Just a few minutes ago. It's hanging right there on that rack." She pointed to a group of clothes. "Is there a problem?"

"I just need to check the pockets," said Alfie. "If you don't mind." He reached into the left pocket. Nothing. Then he reached into the right-hand pocket and pulled out a shiny brass key about three inches long. "Bingo!"

CHAPTER SIX

They biked back to the rectory. Pastor Perkins had just returned.

"Here's your key, Pastor," said Alfie.

Pastor Perkins gave a great sigh. "Thank you, thank you! I *knew* you could find it! I had faith! But where was it?"

Alfie explained.

"Well, of course, that's what I did," said Pastor Perkins. "How forgetful of me." He stopped. "You didn't tell Mrs. Perkins, did you?"

"No, sir. Our lips are sealed," said Betts.

"Tighter than that locked closet."

"Oh, good." Pastor Perkins smiled. "What do I owe you for such good work?"

"We've already been paid," said Alfie. "In cookies."

Back at home, Betts pulled out her notebook.

"Well done, Sherlock," she said.

Then she wrote, 'Missing key mystery cleaned up. Closet opened. Case closed,'

She signed the notebook 'Watson' and put it beside the others on the top shelf of the bookcase.

"I have faith," she said, "that our next mystery will be just as interesting."

The End

THE SECOND STREET SNOOPS AND THE MYSTERY OF THE COLORFUL CAT

Nancy Sweetland

CHAPTER ONE

"Well, we finally got the yard work done," said Betts Binks. "But I'd rather have been working on a case."

Alfie and Betts were spending their summer being detectives like Sherlock Holmes and Doctor Watson.

"Yeah," answered Alfie. "Boy, I'm hot! Let's take a break." He pulled a Game Boy out of his pocket and headed for the swing under the shady oak tree.

Betts sat down, too. "It's been a week since we

found Pastor Perkins' missing key," she said. "What fun is it being detectives without a mystery to solve? Maybe we should put an ad in the paper." Betts gave the swing a push with her foot. "You know, like stores do."

"And say what?" Alfie looked up from his game. "Don't push, it makes me dizzy."

"Oh, you know . . . like our window sign. 'You've Got a Mystery? We'll Make it History!' We could add our number. We need to let people know we're ready for more work." Suddenly she tilted her head and frowned. "Alfie, did you hear that?"

"What?"

"Turn off that noisy game and listen!"

Alfie turned off the game and listened. The yard was quiet except for a light breeze rustling the leaves in the big tree. Then a little hiccupping sound came through the hedge that surrounded the Binks' yard.

"That sounds like . . ." Alfie began.

"Something — or somebody — is in trouble!" finished Betts.

They jumped off the swing. Alfie parted the bushes and they peered through the leaves.

Plump old Mrs. Higbee stood in her yard with tears running down her face. In her arms was a big cat . . . but it didn't look like Digbee, Mrs. Higbee's white angora. This cat wasn't white at all. This cat was lime green, and raspberry red, and lemon yellow, all in splashes . . . and his beautiful fluffy tail was a delicate shade of purple.

Mrs. Higbee held the cat and cried softly. Digbee mewed right along with her.

"Whatever do you suppose has happened to Digbee?" whispered Betts.

"And why is Mrs. Higbee crying?" whispered Alfie.

"Looks like a mystery to me, Sherlock," said Betts. "I've got my notebook in my jeans. Let's check it out."

"Right, Watson." Alfie pushed his Game Boy into his pocket. "A lady in distress is always part of a good mystery."

"And a colorful cat that ought to be white could be the rest of one." They climbed through the hedge into Mrs. Higbee's garden.

CHAPTER TWO

"What's the trouble, Mrs. Higbee?" asked Alfie.

"How can we help?" asked Betts.

"Oh, children! I don't know what's happened to Digbee, just look at him! He's a mess! And the Cat Show is tomorrow! My beautiful Digbee always wins first prize . . . but look at him now!" Mrs. Higbee wailed. "I let him out yesterday and he didn't come back, and when I found him on the step this morning, this is how he looked! Oh, oh, how did this dreadful thing happen?"

Mrs. Higbee pulled a handkerchief from her

apron pocket to blow her nose. "What am I going to do?"

Digbee jumped out of her arms and stalked around on the grass. He rubbed his side against Betts' legs.

She leaned down to pet him. "Oh, he smells good enough to eat! Or drink!"

Alfie picked Digbee up and sniffed. "Lime . . . and . . ." Sniff! "Lemon . . . and . . . raspberry. Maybe cherry?" Sniff, sniff. He shut his eyes. "And his tail is definitely grape. Make a note, Watson. He smells like fruit."

Betts pulled out her notebook and wrote, "Digbee fruity. All colors."

"Have you tried to wash him?" asked Alfie.

"Have I tried! I've tried everything I could think of! And I'm sure you know cats hate to be washed! Nothing works! Digbee is going to be pink and purple for a long time, I'm afraid."

Mrs. Higbee blew her nose again. She shook her grey head. "I guess I'll just have to forget about the Cat Show this year. And I was so hoping to win! The prize is an all expenses paid trip to New York City . . . and I've always wanted to see New York!"

She picked Digbee up. "Come along in, children, and have a cookie. I heard that you were doing some detecting this summer. Maybe you can find out what happened to Digbee."

CHAPTER THREE

Back at their house, Alfie and Betts sat in the swing again to think. How could they find out what happened to Digbee?

Betts dug out her notebook and wrote, 'Digbee victim of color crime.' She said, "Well, it's perfectly obvious that Digbee didn't do that to himself."

"Right."

"So that means somebody did it to him."

"Right again."

"The question is . . ."

"Who. And why."

Betts wrote, 'Who? Why?'

Alfie jumped up. "Holy cow, we forgot! We're supposed to go to the store for Mom! She'll be home in half an hour."

They hopped on their bikes and headed for the grocery.

As Betts started for the dairy section, she suddenly stopped and stared. Mary Alice Blackburn was buying milk, too . . . but she didn't look like the Mary Alice Betts knew. That Mary Alice had hair so blonde it was almost white. This Mary Alice had hair that was all colors . . . green, and yellow, and red . . . and even purple. A delicate shade of purple.

"Mary Alice!" Betts gasped. "What happened to your hair?"

Mary Alice looked down her nose. "For heaven's sake, nothing happened to it. I had it dyed." She turned away.

"My gosh, Betts, make a note!" Alfie

exclaimed, as he walked up. "It's happening to people, too. That's scary."

Betts pulled out her notebook and scribbled, "Scary hair. Mary Alice second color crime victim."

Alfie grinned. "You know Holmes always said, 'The game's afoot?'"

Betts nodded.

"Well, I think this game's ahead."

Betts made a face. "Very funny, Sherlock. But," she paused, "If *we're* going to get ahead, we'd better find out how Mary Alice got rainbowed. And with what?"

"Right. Did you smell her?"

"No, I didn't smell her. But the colors are the same as Digbee's." Betts followed Mary Alice to the bread shelves. "I really love your hair, Mary Alice," Betts said. "Where did you have it done?"

"Go away," said Mary Alice. "My mother is mad at me and I don't want to talk about it."

"Oh, but it's so special. I might want to try it."

"Sure, get yourself in trouble, too. It probably wouldn't work on red hair like yours. Well," Mary Alice sniffed, "I'd like to tell you who did it, but I was sworn to secrecy. Sorry."

"I'm sorry, too, Mary Alice." Betts grinned. "I really do think your hair is something!"

"Yeah. So does my mother," said Mary Alice.

CHAPTER FOUR

"She wouldn't tell me anything, but I think it must have been Jell-O. Or maybe Kool-Aid," said Betts as she put the groceries into the refrigerator. "That's why Digbee smelled so good. Probably just an experiment for fun, I suppose. It didn't hurt him, really."

"Nooo . . . but think about this." Alfie frowned. "What if some jealous cat owner did it to stop her from winning the prize this year? Poor Mrs. Higbee! She really wants to go to New York."

After dinner, Mr. Binks pushed back his chair. "What's up, you two? Usually it's jabber, jabber, at the dinner table. What's the problem? Working on a case, are you?"

Betts and Alfie nodded.

"Going to tell us about it?" Mr. Binks asked.

They did.

He shook his head. "Why would anyone color a cat?"

"That's what we're trying to figure out," said Alfie.

"And poor Mrs. Higbee . . . she had her heart set on going to New York if she won the trip," added Betts.

"Oh, that's too bad," said Mrs. Binks. "Does anyone want dessert?"

Alfie and Betts took their cake out to the swing.

"I've been thinking about somebody trying to sabotage Digbee so they could win the prize," said Betts. "How many cats do we know?"

"Not many. I'm a dog person myself," said Alfie through a mouthful of poppy seed cake.

"It would have to be somebody that lives close enough to Mrs. Higbee to know Digbee," mused Betts.

Alfie nodded. He thought for a minute, then jumped out of the swing. "Come on, Betts! Garbage day is tomorrow."

"So what?"

"Think about it! Whoever dyed Digbee would throw the evidence in the garbage, right?"

"Right!" Betts made a face. "Oh, no! You're not thinking of—"

"Oh, yes, I am. Come on, we haven't got much time. We'll do the cans in the block next to Mrs. Higbee's first."

"Well, you're Sherlock for this case, so I haven't got a choice. But I don't like it."

"You don't have to like it. You just have to do it. Hurry up, we don't have much time before dark."

Alfie took the lid off the first garbage can at the house next door to Mrs. Higbee's. "Phew! This stuff is really smelly. But I figure the evidence will be right on top, because Digbee only got colored yesterday."

"Right. You dig, I make notes," said Betts. She wrote 'Can #1. No evidence.'

They went on to the next. "C'mon, you can help, can't you?" said Alfie. "It will go quicker that way."

"Well . . . all right. But you owe me."

They went on down the alley, looking in one can after another. Betts was writing 'Can #10, no evidence' as they got to end of the block, when Alfie pulled off the lid and yelled "Bingo!" He held up a bunch of empty Kool-Aid packets.

"This is where Sissy and Penny Parker live," said Betts. "Let's check them out."

But they weren't home. "I don't know where they went," said Mrs. Parker. "Look for a couple of weird-colored heads and you'll find them. Dumbest thing they ever did."

"That wasn't much help," said Betts, writing 'Parkers pink and purple too. Mother says dumb.' "These notes aren't going to be much help."

"You never know. Holmes said that sometimes the obvious is the answer," said Alfie. "And we need to keep records. At least, we're pretty sure now who did it to Digbee. We're just not sure why. Look, here they come!"

When the two girls with varicolored hair were close enough, Betts asked sweetly, "Will you color my cat, too?"

"What? Why would anyone color a cat?" said Sissy Parker.

"Wait a minute," said Penny. "You don't even have a cat! What's this all about?"

Alfie said, "You mean you didn't color Mrs. Higbee's cat Digbee like you did your hair?"

Sissy and Penny shook their colorful heads. "You're crazy. Of course not. We like Mrs. Higbee! Only a meanie would do that, especially right now with the cat show on Saturday. Sorry, you Binks will have to detect somewhere else."

Betts wrote, 'Parkers not perpetrators.' "Well, Sherlock?" she said. "Our evidence evidently wasn't conclusive."

"No. But it made me think of something. You know Mr. Ringer? That old man that lives over a block? The one that does odd jobs? He was working on Mrs. Higbee's house a couple of days ago. And . . ." Alfie paused, ". . . if you remember, he had a cat in the show last year."

"Yes, he did! A big black angora. It took second place."

"Uh-huh. Are you thinking what I'm thinking?" Alfie asked.

Betts nodded. "That he just might not want Digbee to win again."

"You got it! Let's go. There's one more garbage can to check."

But Mr. Ringer's garbage can was nowhere in sight in the alley behind his garage.

"I don't like this," whispered Betts. "Besides, it's getting dark."

"We can't give up now," Alfie whispered back. "C'mon, we'll look in the garage."

Betts peered around the corner of the building. "What if he sees us?"

"We'll think of something." Alfie pushed on

the small garage door and jumped back when the rusty hinges screeched open.

"Be quiet!" Betts slipped in behind him and closed the door. "It's really dark. I can hardly see anything."

"Me, either," said Alfie, and tripped over a rake that banged against a metal can and knocked it over. He landed on the floor among papers and bags. Scattered among them were a dozen or more empty packages of Kool-Aid. "But I guess we found the evidence."

The door burst open behind them, and Mr. Ringer stepped in, carrying a baseball bat. "I guess you did," he said in a gravelly voice. "So what are you going to do about it?"

CHAPTER FIVE

Betts drew herself up very straight and said, "Shame on you, Mr. Ringer! You did a very mean thing to Mrs. Higbee."

Mr. Ringer looked surprised. "I didn't do anything to Mrs. Higbee. I did it to Digbee."

"Then you admit it," said Alfie, getting up and brushing the seat of his pants. "You wanted to keep Digbee out of the show."

Mr. Ringer's shoulders slumped. He hung his head and put down the baseball bat. "Yes. And I feel pretty bad about it, too, let me tell you."

Then he stuck out his chin. "But she always wins! If Digbee isn't there, my cat Klinger could take the prize."

"Mrs. Higbee will have to know about this," said Betts. "But maybe she won't do anything . . . if . . ."

"If what?" Mr. Ringer looked hopefully at Betts.

"If you withdraw Klinger from the show."

Mr. Ringer sighed. "I will. It's the least I can do."

At the cat show the next afternoon, Mrs. Higbee was all smiles. Digbee had a big blue ribbon on his basket.

"Did Digbee win after all? Even all colors?" asked Betts.

"Not the big prize. Not this time, like he is," said Mrs. Higbee. "But he won anyway, in a whole new category! Digbee is the most Colorful Cat in the show! And," Mrs. Higbee smiled again,

"I'm going to New York after all! Because he feels so bad about what he did, Mr. Ringer is paying my way!"

Later, after Betts filed her notebook on the top shelf of the bookcase next to the notes from the Case of the Missing Bees, Alfie gave her a high five and said, "Well done, Watson! The Case of the Colorful Cat is closed."

"That it is," said Betts, "but don't forget that next time I'm Sherlock. And we *aren't* going to look for evidence in garbage cans!"

The End

Nancy Sweetland

THE SECOND STREET SNOOPS AND THE MYSTERY OF THE BUFFALO BUTTON

CHAPTER ONE

Alfie and Betts Binks sat on their front steps. In the window behind them hung their large, red-bordered sign:

> DETECTING DONE HERE
>
> The Second Street Snoops
>
> YOU HAVE A MYSTERY?
> WE'LL MAKE IT
> HISTORY!

"We'll be like Sherlock Holmes and Watson," Alfie had told their parents on the first day of summer vacation.

"But we'll take turns being Sherlock," Betts had added. "I'm not doing all the paperwork."

Today was Betts' turn to be Sherlock. "I'm ready for a mystery," she said. "In fact, I think I see one coming now. Look!"

Careening around the corner was a bright green Volkswagen bug painted all over with pictures of buttons. Round buttons, square buttons, buttons like stars. A sign on the side said:

*BUTTON, BUTTON!
WHO'S GOT THE
BUTTON?
BERNIE THE
BUTTON LADY.*

The car screeched to a stop and a short, chunky woman wearing red coveralls and a beret covered with all sorts of bobbling buttons bounced out of the car. "You the Snoops?" she asked, squinting at them.

Alfie and Betts stood up. "Yes, Ma'am," they said together.

"Well, I need some snooping done. Yes, I do. I really do," the woman said. "I'm Bernie the Button Lady. And I have a problem."

CHAPTER TWO

"My prize buffalo button has been boosted," said Bernie the Button Lady.

"Boosted?" asked Alfie.

"As in lifted, stolen, gone," said Bernie, throwing up her arms. "Snatched."

"Take a note, Watson," said Betts.

'Buffalo Button boosted,' wrote Alfie in the case notebook. "Tell us about it."

Bernie sighed and wiggled her plump self down on the steps beside Betts. "It was gone this morning when I opened my display at the

Unusual Animal Show at the fairgrounds." She sniffed and continued. "There's a prize for the most unusual animal pet, the most unusual animal flower, and the most unusual animal button. Collectors come from all over." Her shoulders drooped. "I know my buffalo button should win! But it's gone."

Alfie wrote, 'Buffalo roamed.'

"When did you last see it?" asked Betts.

"It was there when the show closed last night." A tear rolled down Bernie's cheek. "When I got back this morning the whole show was in a terrible mess! Somehow the animals got out during the night and knocked over all the exhibits. Plants uprooted, food bowls tipped over—" She took a deep breath. "When I got my exhibit set up again, my buffalo button was gone."

"How big was it?" asked Betts.

"*Is* it, you mean. I'll draw a picture." Bernie took Alfie's notebook and drew a round button with the shape of a buffalo on it. "It's almost two inches across. It's real shiny brass with a red stone sparkling in the buffalo's eye."

Alfie wrote, 'Red eye. Real shiner.'

Bernie's lip trembled. "It's my very best button. I know it should win the prize, and now it's gone, snatched, lifted."

"Let me call our Mom," said Betts. "Then we'll go with you to the scene of the crime."

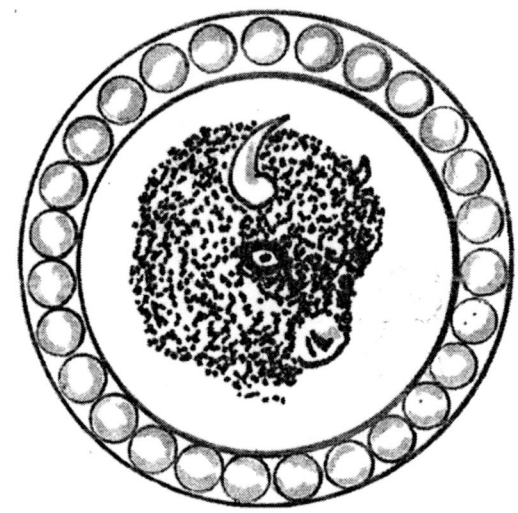

CHAPTER THREE

The fairgrounds pavilion was a mess. It bustled with people catching animals to put them back in cages, repotting plants and setting up button exhibits.

"Wow," said Alfie. "This is interesting! There's a chinchilla and a cage of ferrets. And a white rat with pink eyes!"

"Never mind that other stuff," said Bernie. She pulled them over to the button collections.

"See?" She pointed to an empty spot on one velvet-covered display board. "That's where my buffalo button should be. And it's gone. Just gone."

"Boosted," added Alfie. He liked that word.

"Nothing else missing?" asked Betts.

Bernie shook her head.

Alfie wrote, 'Nothing else missing.'

"The judging is going to start in just one hour," said Bernie. "Please, *please* find my buffalo button!"

CHAPTER FOUR

Betts and Alfie walked slowly around the exhibit hall, looking into every cage and every flowerpot. Nothing.

"How did the animals get out?" Betts asked a man who was holding a baby raccoon.

"I'm pretty sure this fellow got loose and opened the other cages," he said. "Raccoons are very clever with their paws, you know. Good thing the building was locked so none of the animals escaped."

"I'm learning a lot here," Betts said as she

looked at the plant exhibit. "All these flowers have animal names. Hens-and-chicks, goat's beard, even bee balm."

"Interesting, but this isn't helping find that buffalo button," said Alfie, watching a man repotting monkey flowers. "Have you seen any suspicious characters around here this morning?" he asked.

The man frowned. "Nobody but you two. Why?"

"We're looking for a missing button," said Betts.

"For your lip, I hope," said the man crossly. "Don't bother me about buttons. Can't you see I'm a plant man?"

Alfie wrote, 'Don't monkey with the plant man.'

"Whooie," Alfie said as they walked away. "He certainly was no help."

"No," said Betts. "But I have an idea."

CHAPTER FIVE

They went back to Bernie's exhibit. "Have you found my button?" she asked.

"Not yet," said Betts. "But I think we might be able to. Do you have another shiny button?"

Bernie looked through her trays. "Nothing quite as shiny as my buffalo's red eye. But here's one made from copper. Would that do?"

"We'll see. Thanks. Come on, Alfie. We're going to ferret something out."

Alfie frowned. "Farmers used ferrets to get rabbits out of their holes. What's that got to do with buttons?"

"Elementary, Watson," said Betts as they walked back to the animal section. "Excuse me," she said to the ferret's owner. His name tag said, 'Tom.' "Could you assist us with an experiment?"

"Sounds interesting," Tom said. "What can I do to help?"

CHAPTER SIX

"We want to see if it's true that ferrets like to take shiny things," said Betts. "Like buttons, maybe."

Alfie made a note, 'Experiment in progress.'

"Oh, they do," said Tom. "In fact, they'll not only take things, they'll eat almost anything they can find."

"I hope not," said Betts. "Here." She held out Bernie's shiny copper button. "Will you give this to your ferret so we can see what he does with it?"

Tom thought a minute. "I guess it couldn't

hurt, as long as we're watching." He took the button and put it just inside the ferret's cage.

For a moment the ferret looked curiously at the button. Then he snatched it up in his mouth and ran back to the far side of his cage.

"Oh, don't let him eat it!" said Alfie. "Bernie wouldn't forgive us if she lost two buttons!"

"Never fear," said Betts. "See what he's doing?"

The ferret was scrabbling into the cloth of the old shirt that covered the bottom of his cage.

"He's hiding the button," said Tom. "They do that."

Alfie wrote, "Ferret ferreting."

"May I look in his cage?" asked Betts. "He won't bite, will he?"

Tom said, "I'll hold him. What do you expect to find?"

"The solution to a mystery," said Betts. She reached into the cage's rumpled cloth, pulled out the copper button, a piece of aluminum foil –

The Second Street Snoops

and the shiny buffalo button!

CHAPTER SEVEN

"You did it!" Bernie clapped her hands. "You found my buffalo button! I'm so happy!" She hugged them both.

A deep voice crackled over the loudspeaker. "Please take your places. Judging is about to begin."

Bernie's buffalo button won first place.

"Congratulations, Bernie," said Betts. "Make a note, Watson. The mystery of the Buffalo Button is sewn up."

Alfie wrote, 'The ferret did it,' and pushed the

case notebook into his pocket. "Good going, Sherlock," he said. "Case closed. I hope our next mystery is as easy as this one."

The End

Nancy Sweetland

THE SECOND STREET SNOOPS AND THE MYSTERY OF THE MISSING "L"

CHAPTER ONE

Alfie and Betts Binks stood on the sidewalk and looked at the colorful red-bordered sign in the big front window of their house.

Alfie and Betts were spending their summer in the detecting business, taking turns being Sherlock, while Watson kept notes. "Do you think we'll ever get any more detecting business?" asked Betts.

"Sure. Don't forget we've had some successes," said Alfie, looking down the street. "My favorite was finding Mr. Horton's bees.

Well! Here's someone coming right now, and she's seen our sign! Quick, into the office!"

DETECTING DONE HERE

The Second Street Snoops

**YOU HAVE A MYSTERY?
WE'LL MAKE IT
HISTORY!**

Alfie and Betts zipped around the house, through the back door and up to the dining room window where they had put the sign.

"Yes, she's coming here! It's somebody I never saw before," said Alfie. "Get your notebook and look professional, like Watson. I'll let her in."

The lady at the door was very short, no taller than Alfie or Betts. She was also very wide. She could hardly get through the door without turning sideways. "Hello, dears," she said. "I'm Lydia Lynch. I saw your sign. I've got a problem."

"Please come in and sit down," said Betts politely, offering a chair and getting her notebook ready. "Now, how can we help you?"

Lydia Lynch squinted at Alfie and Betts through very thick glasses that made her blue eyes look enormous. "I certainly hope you can help me. You are the Second Street Snoops, aren't you?"

"That's us," said Alfie and Betts together.

"Mrs. Higbee told me all about you," said Lydia Lynch. "And so did Bernie the Button Lady. They were very happy with your work."

"That's nice to hear," said Betts. "Do you have a mystery for us?"

"Well, I certainly do! Someone has stolen my letter L. That is, someone must have. It's simply gone."

"Stolen your letter L? From where?" Alfie

asked, frowning.

"Well, from my typewriter, of course. Let me tell you, it's awfully difficult to write poems without any L's. No 'love,' no 'life,' no 'listen' . . . the list — there's another one — the list is endless, and what am I to do without my L?"

Lydia Lynch wiped away a tear. "I can't even type my name. 'Ydia Ynch' is simply no name for a poet. I do hope you can help. Your sign says you love a mystery, and this certainly is one!"

Alfie and Betts looked at each other. "It certainly is," said Betts. She picked up her notebook and pencil. "Now, when did you see it last?"

"That's the funniest thing," said Lydia Lynch. "I can't remember, for sure. It was there when I wrote the poem about lizards . . . that was Tuesday . . . yes, and it was there yesterday when I wrote about locks . . . that's when I saw it last. Both the capital L and the little L are gone, you know, both of them, as if it weren't bad enough to lose one. Today I tried to write about Lincoln Logs, and all I got was 'blank-i-n-c-o-blank-n blank-o-g-s,' if you can imagine making a poem out of that."

"Not likely,' said Alfie.

"Well, I feel better already," said Lydia Lynch, getting up. "I'll go on home now and let you get to work. But do hurry. I have a wonderful idea for a poem about liberty, and 'iberty' just doesn't work at all!"

CHAPTER TWO

Alfie and Betts watched Lydia Lynch waddle down the walk. "The game's afoot, Betts," said Alfie. "What have you got on your notes?"

Betts looked at her small notebook. "Lydia Lynch. No L."

"That's all?"

Betts looked at her notebook again. "Last seen yesterday."

Alfie nodded, squeezing his eyes tight shut.

"Why are you doing that?"

"It makes me think better," he said. "Where

shall we look?"

"Who would steal an L? And, if they did, what would they do with it?" Betts mused. "I certainly would have no use for one without the other twenty-five letters."

"Cookies help me think better, too," said Alfie. "Let's get some. Or as Lydia Lynch would have to write now, 'ets get some'!"

They sat in the big backyard swing munching chocolate chip cookies. "Observation is very important in a case like this," said Betts. "Did you notice that Lydia Lynch has very bad eyes?"

"That's right," said Alfie. "That L could be anywhere, and she wouldn't know it. Let's go have a look in her house."

"Good idea," said Betts.

Lydia Lynch let them in. "Hello, dears! Have you solved my mystery already?"

"Not yet, Miss Lynch," said Alfie. "We're working on it."

The whole house was a jumble. Boxes and

newspapers were everywhere. "I hate to throw anything away, you see," she explained. "I like old things."

"You search the kitchen, Betts," Alfie said. "I'll take the living room."

Lydia Lynch said, "Oh, I do hope you find my L. I'm blank-o-s-t without it!"

CHAPTER THREE

Alfie pulled his magnifying glass from his pocket. "Just give us a little time, please."

He began to go over all the piled up papers stacked on a table. "There's lots of L's in these," he said.

"But not my L," said Lydia Lynch.

"Nothing in the kitchen," announced Betts. "Lots of L's, though, on all the food boxes."

"But not my L," Lydia Lynch said again.

"There's only one place it could be," said Alfie. "We'd like to have a look at your typewriter."

"Please," added Betts.

"Of course. Squeeze through here."

Lydia Lynch took them into a room that was crowded with chairs and small tables, dusty lampshades and piles and piles of books.

They followed her through a maze of boxes and cushions and piled-up magazines, around a tall hutch and back to a small, rickety table. Like everything else in the room, the typewriter was very old.

"Look at this, Alfie," said Betts. "All the keys on this typewriter are out of line."

"I see," said Alfie. "But are they all there?" He peered through his magnifying glass.

"Oh, my," said Lydia Lynch. "How clever you are! I would never have thought to look through a glass like that."

Alfie moved the glass slowly above the top of the typewriter. "Aha!"

Alfie looked at Betts. Betts looked at Alfie.

"I believe we've solved your problem," said

Betts. "Just let me bend this a little bit." She worked with the typewriter for a moment, lining up the L with the other letters in the machine. "May I have a piece of paper?"

"Of course." Lydia Lynch gave Betts a clean piece of paper. Betts wound it into the machine and moved over so Alfie could stand in front of it. "Alfie's the typist in the family," she explained.

Alfie put his fingers on the keys and typed, 'Life is lovely and worth living.' The L's were all there.

"Well, my goodness!" said Lydia Lynch, squinting at the paper. "How did you solve the mystery so quickly?"

Betts looked at Alfie and grinned. Alfie looked at Betts and grinned back. Then, in the tradition of Holmes and Watson, they said together, "It was L-ementary!"

The End

Nancy Sweetland

THE SECOND STREET SNOOPS AND THE CASE OF THE DISAPPEARING DINOSAUR EGG

CHAPTER ONE

"I'll be back to pick you up," said Mrs. Binks as Alfie and Betts jumped out of the car at the museum. "Behave yourselves and don't get into any trouble."

"Trouble?" said Alfie and Betts together. "Us?"

"Yes, you," Mrs. Binks laughed. "Somehow, your curiosity seems to work overtime."

"We just want to see the animated dinosaurs again, Mom," said Betts.

"Yeah," added Alfie. "Anyway, what could

happen in a museum?"

They followed big green painted dinosaur tracks leading through the museum's glass doors and up the stairs, where growly roars echoed off the museum walls.

Suppose they really sounded like that?" asked Betts, rubbing the goose bumps on her arms.

"I guess," Alfie said. "Pretty scary."

Inside the exhibit, a huge Alamosaurus nodded its massive head and chewed tall grass. Its long tail slashed back and forth. An enormous Tyrannosaurus reared up, tearing the air with clawed two-fingered hands. Its roar showed a mouthful of jagged teeth.

"Wow," breathed Betts, reading the sign. "This weighed seven tons! I thought horses were pretty big. I don't know about you, but I'm glad these guys are extinct."

They looked at bony-plated plant eaters with clubbed tails, and marine lizards called Platecarpus. They gawked at Triceratops and Brontosaurus, and finally stopped at a waist-high exhibit of a Protoceratops' nest, where long, rounded eggs lay in a shallow depression of sand.

"Protoceratops were only about six feet long," read Alfie. "Do you suppose those eggs are real?"

"Real fossils." Betts frowned. "Say, weren't there six whole eggs in this nest last week?"

Alfie wrinkled his forehead. "Yeah. And look! One's broken! I don't remember that!

Betts leaned over the railing to see more closely. Suddenly a heavy hand grabbed her shoulder.

"You should know better," growled a big museum guard. "No touching the exhibits."

"I'm sorry," said Betts. "But one of the eggs is broken! It was whole last week,"

"Honest," said Alfie. "It was."

The guard's eyes narrowed at Betts. "Not likely. I saw you messing with that exhibit. You must have broken it when I wasn't looking."

"I wouldn't do any such thing!" Betts said indignantly.

"No back talk. You'd better come with me." The guard angrily pushed Alfie and Betts downstairs, where tall, thin Mr. Kieper, the museum director, sat behind a large desk covered with papers and thick, important-looking books.

"Well, if it isn't some of my best customers." He smiled as he peered over his half-glasses. "What can I do for the Binks twins this afternoon?"

"She broke a dinosaur egg, Mr. Kieper," said the guard, pointing down at Betts. "I practically saw her do it."

"You know she wouldn't do that, Mr. Kieper," said Alfie.

"Of course she wouldn't. Now, what's this all about?"

Betts told him about the cracked-open egg.

"Ridiculous!" Mr. Kieper slapped his hand on

the desk. "No one is allowed to touch the exhibits. Everybody knows that. I put that particular display together myself and all the eggs were just fine."

"Well they're not just fine now," said Betts. "One of them has hatched!"

CHAPTER TWO

"Look at this!" Mr. Kieper poked his bony finger at the cracked shell. "This egg shell is certainly not old. And it's most certainly *not* a dinosaur egg."

Alfie pulled his small notebook and pencil from his jeans pocket. "Looks like a mystery to me," he whispered to Betts. "Your turn to handle the case, Sherlock."

"Right, Watson. Make a note."

Alfie wrote, 'Dino egg gone. Fake egg broken.'

"What kind of an egg is it?" he asked the curator.

"I don't know." Mr. Kieper moved half of the empty shell with the tip of his pencil. "It's more round, but about the right size for a Protoceratops egg. It's been painted to match the real fossils. And it certainly does look like something did hatch from it . . . and very recently."

Alfie wrote, 'Egg too round. Painted. Mr. Kieper agrees hatched.'

Betts took a deep breath. "Mr. Kieper, we're detectives, in case you didn't know." She handed him one of their hand-lettered business cards.

> DETECTING DONE HERE
> The Second Street Snoops
> YOU HAVE A MYSTERY?
> WE'LL MAKE IT HISTORY!

Mr. Kieper adjusted his glasses and examined the card. He raised his eyebrows. "Well! I did hear you've had some success with solving little mysteries, but I'm afraid this is going to take someone a lot more experienced." He placed the halves of the painted, broken shell carefully in his handkerchief. "Run along now and don't bother me. I've got to find the real dinosaur egg. It's priceless! And it belongs to the traveling exhibit! They'll have my head!"

Mr. Kieper hurried away. The guard stayed, watching Betts and Alfie with narrowed eyes.

Betts whispered, "Make a note, Watson."

"Right, Sherlock." Alfie wrote, 'Dino egg priceless. Exhibit will have Kieper's head.'

The guard asked suspiciously, "What's that you're writing?"

"Oh, nothing important," said Alfie, stuffing the notebook back in his pocket.

Betts examined the dinosaur nest as well as possible from behind the railing. "Look at those marks in the sand."

Betts pointed to faint scratches that disappeared over the edge of the exhibit.

"Tracks."

"Maybe . . . but what kind?" said Alfie.

"That's what we have to find out."

"You don't have to find out anything." The guard grabbed Betts' and Alfie's arms and roughly pushed them toward the stairs. "It's closing time . . . so out you go!"

He followed them all the way to the door. "And stay out! Bothersome nosy kids!"

Mrs. Binks was waiting in the car. "Did you have a good time?" Then she looked closely at their faces. "Oh, oh! Something's up. Don't tell me you hatched up a mystery in the museum!"

"Let's say you're egg-zactly right," said Alfie.

"And that's no yoke," added Betts.

"Oh, dear," sighed Mrs. Binks. "Why did I ask?"

CHAPTER THREE

The next afternoon Alfie and Betts went to the museum just before closing and asked Mr. Kieper whether he had found the missing dinosaur egg.

"No," he said sadly. "I haven't a clue. I don't want to bring the police into this. I just want the egg back before the exhibit packs up next week."

"Someone left the painted egg so you wouldn't know the real one was missing," said Betts.

"Yes," Mr. Kieper agreed. "But who? Who would want a dinosaur egg? And was there really something in the egg they left?"

"We'll try to find out, if you don't mind," said Betts. "We're good detectives."

"In the tradition of Holmes and Watson," added Alfie. "We have a successful record of solving mysteries."

Mr. Kieper sighed. "Children, children, detect all you want. Just don't bother the museum's patrons. Don't bother the guards. And don't bother me."

Betts and Alfie said, "Yes, sir!" together. Out in the hall they grinned and gave each other a high five.

"Okay, Watson," said Betts, checking her watch. "The museum closes in five minutes. You know the plan."

Alfie nodded. "We hide until everyone's gone, then go to the scene of the crime."

"Right. Got the flashlight?"

Alfie nodded and disappeared into a cleaning supply closet. Betts hid in the ladies' rest room.

A few minutes later someone opened the door, said, "Closing time!" and snapped off the light. Betts waited to be sure everyone was gone before she felt her way out. She stepped into the dark hall and gasped as a bright light hit her in the face.

"Relax, it's only me," Alfie said. "Everyone's gone. Let's go upstairs."

The inside of the museum was black as a moonless night except for the dim glow of the red EXIT sign at the end of the hall.

"It's too quiet in here," whispered Betts.

"Yeah. Creepy." Alfie shone the light on the painted dinosaur tracks leading to where the enormous dinosaurs, silent now, lurked in the shadows. Alfie suddenly flashed the light up on the jagged teeth of Tyrannosaurus Rex.

Betts shivered and grabbed his arm. "Don't do that! It's even more ferocious now than in the daytime!"

"Sorry. Couldn't resist."

Their whispers echoed eerily through the empty building as they continued soundlessly on their rubber-soled shoes through the dark toward the Protoceratops' nest.

Betts shone the light on the display. Everything looked the same except for the broken shell that Mr. Kieper had taken away.

"Now," she said, "as Sherlock would surmise, something came out of that egg."

"And as Watson would agree, you're right."

"It certainly wasn't a dinosaur."

"Certainly not."

"Whatever it was, it had to go somewhere."

"Right again."

Betts squatted down. "Look, here on the floor."

"That's just some sand off the exhibit."

"I know . . . but I think it fell off whatever came out of the egg. See . . ." she crawled along the floor, shining the light ahead, ". . . here's more . . . and here . . ." The sand stopped near the wall.

Alfie followed, moving his notebook into the light to write, 'Sand on floor. More sand on floor.' Then, 'No more sand on floor.'

Suddenly Betts stopped and put her hand on Alfie's arm. "Listen!"

CHAPTER FOUR

"Hear that?" Betts whispered.

Alfie frowned. "No. What?"

Out of the dark came a small sound.

"That!" said Betts.

They crouched, unmoving, for what seemed a long time before they heard it again.

"Sounds like a little bird," said Alfie. "But it sounds funny."

"Like it's echoing in a tin box," said Betts. "Listen, there it is again!" She shone the light along the floor to a heating duct, where something moved under the wide grate. "It *is* a bird," said Betts.

"Yeah, but what kind?" Alfie pulled the grate up and picked up a long-necked, dusty, fluffy puffball. "It's too big for a chicken chick."

"And its neck is too long."

The bird pecked at Alfie's hand.

"It's hungry, too," said Betts. "Probably nearly starved. Let's get out of here. We've solved half the mystery. We know what came out of the egg. Now, if we find where the egg came from—"

Alfie finished, "That will lead us to the rest of the mystery." He slipped the little bird inside his shirt and they tiptoed back to the stairs.

"So far so good. But how do we get out of here without setting off the alarm?" asked Betts. "We should have thought about that."

Just then a key rattled in the door below them. They crouched down at the top of the stairs. Someone turned on the lights.

"It's Mr. Kieper," whispered Betts. "He's

going into his office."

"C'mon!" Alfie zipped down the stairs on his rubber-soled tennies, with Betts right behind him. They slipped quietly out the unlocked door.

"Whew!" Alfie said when they stopped running a block away.

"Double whew," said Betts, gasping for breath. "Lucky."

Alfie grinned. "Double lucky. But you know what Dad says, 'Luck is mostly good timing.'"

Betts looked at her watch. "Talk about timing, it's just six o'clock and Mom and Dad are at that dinner for the Friends of the Zoo. If anybody in this town would know what kind of bird we've got, that person would be there, too!"

"Good thinking, Sherlock. Let's go."

CHAPTER FIVE

"Oh, oh," whispered Mrs. Binks to Mr. Binks as Alfie and Betts appeared at the restaurant door. "I think we've got company."

Mr. Binks raised his eyebrows. "Now, what in the world would the detectives be doing here? Excuse us, please," he said to the other diners. "We'll be right back."

"Sorry, Dad and Mom," said Alfie, "but we need to know what kind of baby bird we have here."

He held out the little ball of fluff that blinked

and opened its mouth. Its head bobbed on its long neck.

"Where in the world did you get that?" asked Mrs. Binks. "I've never seen anything like it."

Mr. Binks frowned. "Neither have I. But I'll bet Mr. Boze will know. He's the head of the bird exhibits. I'll get him."

Mr. Boze did know. He rubbed his hands in his excitement. "My stars, children, that's an emu chick! Wherever did you get it?"

Alfie made a note, "Chick is Emu. Boze knows."

"It's a long story, Mr. Boze," said Betts. "But what's important is, who will take care of it?"

"Well, I will, of course. I have a special case for chicks at the Zoo." He frowned. "We did have an emu nest, but the only egg in it disappeared. Oh, what a drawing card this will be!"

Mr. Boze cradled the little bird in his hands. "I'll take it there right now. The poor thing looks half starved! Oh, thank you, children."

He put it under his suit coat. "Come by the Zoo and visit your emu any time!" he called as he hurried out the door.

"Well!" Mrs. Binks said.

"Well, well," Mr. Binks said.

"Well done!" said Alfie and Betts together, backing out the door. "Have a nice dinner!"

They reviewed Alfie's notes as they walked home.

"Nothing here to solve the mystery of who took the real egg," he said. "Or why."

"No... but I've been thinking. Only someone at the zoo could get an emu egg. Make a note, Watson."

Alfie wrote, 'Who at Zoo took egg from emu?' He read his note aloud to Betts. "Hey, that's almost a poem!"

She made a face. "Robert Frost you aren't. Tomorrow we'll check out the zoo guards' uniforms."

Chapter SIX

The next day when Mr. Binks went to work at the Bank and Mrs. Binks went to volunteer at the library, Alfie and Betts rode their bikes to the Zoo.

Mr. Boze was delighted to see them. "The little emu is doing beautifully. I'm so glad you found him. Tell me now, where was he?"

"It's a long story, Mr. Boze," said Betts. "But if you have a list of the zoo guards' names, I think we can tell you the whole story very soon. Don't the zoo guards and the museum guards wear the same uniforms?"

"Why, yes, they do. Sometimes they trade around." Mr. Boze pulled a list from his files and handed it to Betts. "Is this what you need?"

"I think so," said Betts, reading down the names. Suddenly she stopped. "All right! Thanks, Mr. Boze! See you later! C'mon, Alfie."

"Come on where?"

"To Joey Weathers' house." Betts hopped on her bike.

"The dinosaur freak? The only kid in our class who speaks dinosaur language?" Alfie had to pedal fast to keep up with Betts. "The kid who paints dinosaurs on everything he owns? The one who had the measles so bad he couldn't get out of bed to go see the exhibit? Why are we going there?"

"Because," said Betts, "that's where the dinosaur egg is, I'll bet my allowance."

Alfie shook his head and followed Betts up the Weathers' driveway.

"Please may we visit Joey?" Betts asked a surprised Mrs. Weathers.

"Why, I guess so. He isn't contagious any more. Come in."

Joey was watching television in bed. His face and arms were still covered with spots.

Alfie said "Hi, Joey."

Betts said, "Okay, where is it?"

Joey's face got red all around his spots. "I was going to put it back, honest! I just wanted to see it, a real dinosaur egg. You know I couldn't go to the exhibit."

"Yes, but your plan backfired," said Betts. "When the emu egg hatched."

"It hatched?" Joey said. "Really?"

Alfie shook his head. "I'm lost here. Fill me in, Sherlock."

Betts explained, "Joey's dad is a guard at the Zoo. He knew Joey wanted more than anything to see the dinosaur exhibit, but he couldn't because of the measles. So his dad told Joey he would get one of the eggs — am I right, so far? —" Betts waited for Joey's nod before she went on, "— just for a couple of days. Then he would put it back before the exhibit left town. He brought an emu egg from the zoo that would be just about the right size, and Joey painted it to match the old fossil eggs. But then the emu egg hatched."

Joey reached under his pillow and pulled out the real dinosaur egg. "I wasn't going to keep it, honest!" He was almost crying. "I just wanted to see it, hold it! I know it was wrong. Please, take it back!"

CHAPTER SEVEN

Mr. Kieper looked up over his half glasses as Betts laid the real dinosaur egg on his desk. "You found it? How? Where?" He picked up the egg and cradled it in his hands. "You really are detectives! Who took it? Where was it? Who's to blame?"

Betts said seriously, "Mr. Kieper, if we tell you that the egg was never really stolen, only borrowed, would you let it go at that?"

Mr. Kieper scrunched up his face. "Do I have your word they never intended to keep it?"

Alfie and Betts nodded solemnly.

Mr. Kieper sighed. "Yes."

"All's well and all that," said Betts later. "The Case of the Disappearing Dinosaur Egg is closed."

"Yes," said Alfie, putting the case notebook next to the others on the top shelf of the bookcase. "Good sleuthing, Sherlock. But what was the clue that led you to Joey?"

Betts grinned. "As soon as I saw Mr. Weathers' name on the list of zoo guards, the Case of the Disappearing Dinosaur Egg just came . . . unscrambled!"

The End

Nancy Sweetland

THE SECOND STREET SNOOPS AND THE MYSTERY OF THE STICKS IN THE SANCTUARY

CHAPTER ONE

"Up and at 'em, Snoops," Mr. Binks called up the stairs. "It's clean the church day and your Sunday School class is next up for the job."

Betts rolled over and pulled her pillow over her head. "No mystery there," she mumbled. "Sweep, dust, polish, put the hymn books back in the holders. It's a summer Saturday and we could be doing something more interesting."

She pulled on her jeans and a T-shirt and headed downstairs.

Alfie was already at the table. "Anything

missing this morning except your smile?" he asked, spreading jam on toast already slathered with peanut butter.

"Aren't you funny," Betts said. "After we get done at church, want to do something fun?"

Mrs. Binks poured a glass of orange juice and set it in front of Betts. "Like what would that be?" she asked.

"Maybe go swimming," said Betts. "Or play ball at the park." She poured milk on her Cheerios. "We haven't had a mystery to work on since the missing dinosaur egg, and that was days ago. I said it before and I'll say it again, we should advertise."

Mr. Binks raised his eyebrows.

Mrs. Binks raised hers, too.

Alfie raised his toast and took a big bite.

Betts wrinkled her nose. "Well, *that* fell on deaf ears." She pointed her spoon at the red-bordered sign in the front window.

> **DETECTING DONE HERE**
>
> **The Second Street Snoops**
>
> **YOU HAVE A MYSTERY?
> WE'LL MAKE IT
> HISTORY!**

"Maybe we just need a bigger sign." She finished her cereal.

Alfie pushed back his chair and got up. "C'mon, Betts. If everyone shows up, the cleaning shouldn't take long." He put his dishes in the sink. "Let's go get it over with. Race you to the church."

"You're on." They pedaled down the street as fast as they could.

"I won," puffed Betts, skidding to a stop in

front of the church.

"Not by much," said Alfie.

"Doesn't matter, a win's a win . . ." her voice was cut off by a shriek from inside the church.

CHAPTER TWO

They pushed their bikes into the rack, tumbled off and raced into the dimly-lit sanctuary.

"What's going on?" asked Alfie.

"Billy's putting sticks in my hair," wailed Mary Alice Blackburn. "Off the dirty floor." She bent over and shook her blonde hair that was still a little streaked with raspberry color. A dozen tiny sticks fell out. "Eeeew!" She shivered.

"How'd the sticks get into the church?" asked Betts.

"Probably tracked in on a shoe. Along with

who knows *what* else." Mary Alice glared at Billy Barton.

He smirked. "You Snoops are so smart," he said, "you tell *us* where the sticks came from. I already swept this floor before you got here."

"Not very well, obviously," said Alfie. He held the dustpan for Betts to sweep up the sticks, then dumped them into the wastebasket. "So we're all here. Let's get organized. Who's doing the dust detail?"

"Sissy and I will," said Stacey Jones, picking up a cloth. "We'll dust the pews first, and then Billy and Trevor can polish them. Betts and Mary Alice can clean the altar area."

"Glad to," said Mary Alice, making a face at Billy. "Anything to keep away from *you*."

"I think he likes you, Mary Alice," whispered Betts as they walked up the aisle.

"He has a funny way of showing it."

"That's just boys," said Betts. "Even Alfie is weird sometimes."

CHAPTER THREE

"Everybody get busy and we'll be done in no time," said Alfie. He handed Trevor and Billy cans of furniture spray. "I'll work on the choir loft."

The sanctuary was quiet except for the sssst! of spray polish and swishing cloths rubbing over wood.

"Let's sing while we work," said Sissy. "We can practice for Kid's Choir. That Sunday's coming up soon and we don't sound too great yet."

"Good idea! I know just the song to start with," called Alfie from the choir loft, waving his polishing cloth like a conductor with a baton. "How's this?" He began, "This little church of mine...I'm gonna make it shine..."

"Cool!" said Sissy, "C'mon, everyone!"

They all chimed in and the church echoed with their voices. "This little church of mine . . . I'm gonna make it shine . . . make it shine . . . make it shine . . . make it shine!"

Just then the Pastor's wife came in carrying a big bouquet of sparkling white and yellow daisies. "How wonderful to hear you all singing!" Mrs. Perkins gave the flowers to Mary Alice. "Throw those wilted lilies out and replace them on the altar with these. I brought some of my Heavenly chocolate chip cookies—" she paused and smiled up at Alfie "—for everyone when you've finished."

She set a plate piled high with cookies on a table near the door. As she went out she said,

"God's birds couldn't sing any sweeter!"

The church began to sparkle as they sang "Jesus Loves Me" and all the verses of "Amazing Grace."

"Who's up for a pick-up ball game at the park, after?" asked Trevor.

"After what?" asked Stacey.

"After cookies," said Billy. "How about you, Blondie?" he asked Mary Alice.

"The name is Mary Alice, Silly Billy," she said, tossing her head, "and yes, I'm up for a game. I think we're done here."

She threw her dust cloth into the pile in the janitor's closet. The others did the same and went out, except for Betts, who stopped in the aisle and looked down.

"I don't believe it!" she said.

CHAPTER FOUR

"I thought I cleaned these up," she said as she frowned at a few little twigs on the floor. "Guess I missed some." She quickly swept them up.

They all biked to the park and played ball until Alfie said, "Let's go home, Betts. It's time for a lunch munch."

"I agree," she said. "But I have to stop by the church on the way home. I left my sweatshirt on one of the pews."

"Okay, but let's hurry. I'm starving."

They pushed open the church door. "Wow,

doesn't it smell clean!" exclaimed Alfie. "We did a good job."

Betts picked her sweatshirt up off a pew and said, "Maybe not. Look, more sticks. Maybe what *I* smell is a mystery."

"And it's afoot," said Alfie, kicking the twigs.

"Cut that out! It's my turn to be Sherlock, and *I* get to say that," grumbled Betts.

Alfie grinned. "So say it."

Betts made a face at him and said, "The game's afoot," in her best imitation of Sherlock Holmes. She got the broom and dustpan and was sweeping again when Pastor Perkins came in.

"Ah!" he said. "I was hoping to catch you both here. It looks as though you've already started working on my mystery."

"What mystery is that, Pastor?" asked Alfie.

Pastor Perkins sighed. "It's those sticks. Every day there are a few more. We sweep them up and the next day they're here again. You two did such a good job finding my missing key, maybe you can figure this out. I do hope so." He went into the church office.

"Now it's official. It feels good to have a mystery again," said Betts. "Make a note, Watson."

"It will feel even better to solve it," said Alfie, putting the sticks into the garbage can in the janitor's closet. He pulled a new notebook from his pocket and labeled it, "The Sticks in the Sanctuary Mystery." Then he turned to new page and wrote, 'Sticks swept up. More every day. Pastor Perkins counting on us.' He put the notebook back in his pocket. "C'mon, Betts. We can think better when we're not hungry."

CHAPTER FIVE

At home they found a note on the kitchen table. "Gone shopping. Make a sandwich. Have an apple."

"PB and J?" asked Betts, reaching for the bread.

"Always room for peanut butter," said Alfie.

They took their sandwiches and milk to the sun-dappled backyard and sat in the big wooden swing. Birds tweeted and twittered in the trees. They could hear Mrs. Higbee talking to her cat Digbee in the next yard.

Betts gave the swing a push with her foot. "I've been thinking, Watson," she said through a mouthful.

"I'll make a note of that." He pulled his notebook from his jeans and wrote, 'Sherlock thinking. Could be scary.'

Betts punched his arm. "*That's* not an official note! Erase it."

"Can't." He grinned and held up his stubby pencil. "No eraser."

"I really did sweep up those sticks."

"I know. I helped."

"But Pastor Perkins said they keep coming back. So where do they come from?"

"*That's* for us to find out. Right now, I'm going to look up that bird." He pointed to a small shadow flitting about in the hedge.

"That's just a sparrow. You know sparrows."

"Yeah, but what kind? There are, for your information, my dear detective, many different kinds of sparrows. I've identified four just in our yard."

"Have at it, then," said Betts, getting up. "I'm going to work on tomorrow's Sunday School lesson. We're supposed to find a Bible verse that has some meaning to our lives today."

"Look up one that has to do with sparrows," said Alfie.

Betts laughed. "Sure, Watson." Then she stopped, stood still and snapped her fingers. "Alfie! That's it! I've solved the case!" She paused. "Maybe."

Alfie frowned. "Just like that?"

"I think so. Let's go back to the church. I have an idea."

"Clue me in."

"I will when we get there. Come on!"

Afternoon sunshine streamed through the stained glass windows, illuminating the big sanctuary.

"I knew it!" Betts said, pointing down. "More sticks. Make a note, Watson."

"So?" Alfie frowned, but he wrote, 'Snoops return to cleaned scene. More sticks.' Then he said, "I give. Explain, Sherlock."

"Actually, *you* solved the mystery," said Betts, smiling, "when you told me to look up a Bible verse on sparrows."

Alfie shrugged and shook his head.

"Don't you get it?" Betts pointed to the high, dark vaulted ceiling. "Look up, like you said!"

Alfie wrinkled his forehead but he wrote, 'Look up is clue?'

"A sparrow is making a nest way up on that rafter," said Betts. "See? There must be a hole in the roof where she gets in." Just then a small twig fell on Alfie's head and a fluffy little feather floated down through the sunlight. "But she's not a very good nest-maker. Get it?"

"Got it!" Alfie shook the twig off his hair, grinned and gave Betts a high-five. "She keeps losing her nesting stuff. Good work, Sherlock!" Alfie wrote, 'Sloppy sparrow. Drops sticks.' He slipped the notebook back into his pocket. "Let's go tell Pastor Perkins."

CHAPTER SIX

"A sparrow?" asked the Pastor. "Building a nest in my church? Really! We'll have to take it down." He thought for a moment, then shook his head. "No. In Luke chapter twelve sparrows are mentioned."

He reached for his Bible and flipped a few pages. "Here it is. It says, 'Not one of them is forgotten before God.' We will just let Mrs. Sparrow keep building. After the baby birds are gone I'll have the janitor clean the nest away and find the hole where she comes in. What do a few little sticks matter when one of God's creatures needs a home?" Pastor Perkins smiled. "Thanks, Snoops! You not only solved the mystery, you gave me a subject for my next sermon!"

Later, back at home, Alfie wrote, 'Case closed,' and filed the Sticks in the Sanctuary Mystery next to the others on the top shelf in the bookcase. "That was quick work, Sherlock," he said. "It was a very stick-y case."

Betts made a face at him. "Right. One more mystery solved." Then she grinned. "How tweet it is!"

Alfie groaned. "Next time *I'm* Sherlock. And we *don't* need to advertise. Mysteries just keep winging our way!"

The End

Made in the USA